# Greenspell:
# A Fantasy Anthology

## By Kathy Ann Trueman

Writers Exchange E-Publishing

http://www.writers-exchange.com

Greenspell: A Fantasy Anthology
Copyright 2005 Kathy Ann Trueman
Writers Exchange E-Publishing
PO Box 372
ATHERTON QLD 4883

Cover Art by: Odile Stamanne

Published by Writers Exchange E-Publishing
http://www.writers-exchange.com

# The Sow's Ear

Janell could feel the magic building in power, resisting, tingling up her arms, almost snarling at her as she began the first unraveling of its threads of energy. This curse spell was strong and complex, astonishingly so. She pulled back slightly, not discouraged, but needing to breathe and review the task.

Across the sparsely furnished room, her customer sat sulking. She was a plain, lumpy woman, well into her middle age, but not ugly. When Janell had asked why she wanted to pay so dearly to have her curse removed, the woman had gestured down at her body with contempt. "Look at me!" she had shouted. "I was beautiful, graceful, fertile! I can't go on living in this hideous, useless body!"

Janell could understand that. She wasn't beautiful herself, but she chose to appear that way, and she knew the benefits and seductions of beauty. "Why did the mage curse you?" was her next question.

"He wanted my treasure. Now he has it, or most of it." The woman stared forlornly down at work-roughened hands. "But he's taken away the only thing I truly valued. I want that back. I want to be what I was before he cursed me." Then she pulled out a pouch and emptied its contents on the table before Janell. "Here is all I was able to come away with. I give it all to you, to remove this curse and make me beautiful again."

The pile of jewels glittered at Janell. If this was only a portion, no wonder the mage had been willing to curse her to get the rest! Further, Janell could see that one of the gems, a ruby amulet, was ensorcelled. Unable to resist, she ran her fingers through the stones, then lifted the amulet. There was no obvious clue to what kind of spell was on it.

The woman stared at her anxiously. She was no mage, and Janell began to think she didn't realize what she had here. She pretended to be bored, asking, "Where did you come by such a treasure?"

Without the least hint of shame, even with pride, the woman said, "My father was a great thief. And a great miser." Then, "Is it enough?"

The gems represented more than Janell could make with ten such spell-castings, even without the ensorcelled ruby. She couldn't wait to begin to decipher the amulet's resident magic. Still, she hadn't lost all caution. Her own spells, cast on this room, not only told her this was no rival mage seeking to attack her while she concentrated, but also whether or not the woman was telling a lie. When Janell checked, she saw the woman had spoken only the truth.

The decision was easy. Janell made the slight gesture to raise the room's protective shields, which would prevent any interruption once she began. "It is enough," she said. "Barely. I will help you." And she warned the woman not to speak, not to move until the curse was broken.

Now she was deeply into it, following and picking apart the threads of energy as a tailor might pick apart seams. Even for a shapechanging spell it was complex, going off in unexpected directions, strong where it should have been weak and weak where she might have made it strong. But this was what she was best at, and she followed it all the way to its heart. When she had it, the core of light from which the rest had been born, she held it in two magical "hands", contained it, and then sent her own counterspell into its center like a knife.

The woman threw back her head and began to scream, but Janell wasn't startled. Shapechanging always involved some pain, and forced shapechanging even more. She kept her attention on the curse, fracturing it and blowing away the pieces, letting them join the energy ambient in the room. It was done.

The woman had fallen forward, hunched over herself in the chair, the scream beginning to change into another sound. Janell was already reaching for the amulet when she realized the sound wasn't the weeping that usually followed a shapechange. It was a growl, soft, but building abruptly into a roar. The roar filled Janell's ears, filled the room, until the very air vibrated with the crescendo as if unable to hold it. It wasn't a roar of pain, but of triumph. Janell flinched back, rising, stumbling backward over her chair.

In seconds, the woman's plain clothing and sallow skin melted away, and a shape unfolded that was much, much larger, richly black and shining with iridescence, as if it had feasted on colors and kept them trapped in the blackness, allowing them to play along curves as it rose and continued to rise. A long neck unfolded, arched like a swan's to keep the long reptilian head from grazing the ceiling. The body lengthened, filling the room from right to left, a tail sweeping around until it almost touched Janell. Thick muscular legs tipped with long golden claws crushed the chair beneath it, and black wings spread from the shoulders, opening on a frame of bony elongated fingers, like a bat's.

*The spells! She can't have lied to me without my knowing!* Janell thought in panic, and then she realized. The woman said her true form had been young and beautiful. She never said it had been *human.*

Her true form was beautiful, but it was a beauty of towering, glittering grace and raw strength, as terrible as thunderclouds rolling to fill the sky with tossed blackness and flashing lightning. Inhumanly perfect curves shuddered, stretched, shook off the last construction of its cursed form, and settled with the inevitability of the first whisper of an avalanche.

It was done. The head swung around to face Janell, the eyes red and flickering. They weren't human eyes, but Janell could still see the gleeful triumph in them. She tried desperately to cast a spell to protect herself as the mouth opened, showing rows of long teeth. But the dragon didn't bite her. It said, "Arlahalimin."

Now, horrified, Janell knew what the amulet did. *"No!"* she screamed, the protest tearing from her throat, but it was much too late. The room and the dragon seemed to rush away from her as she sank, became small, then smaller and smaller--

She saw the dragon through a red haze. She was inside the amulet.

The dragon rested its head on the table with a contented grumble that made the wood tremble, almost knocking Janell to her knees within the tiny room that was the inside of the ruby. "Now I go to take back my treasure," she said. Teeth glinted with her smile. "And you will help me. In that amulet, you have no choice but to obey me. You will fight the mage with magic, because I cannot. If you fail, you shall die," she pointed out unnecessarily. "But if you win..." A claw hooked the amulet's chain, and Janell was swept dizzyingly up into the air.

"If you win," the dragon said, still smiling, "you shall be the pride of my collection."

# Thief from Thief

(a sequel to "The Sow's Ear")

Janell closed the contact with the thread of verdal magic and sat down, dejected, chin in her hands. Another dead end. It was hopeless. Three years, four months, and fifteen days she had been a prisoner in this ruby amulet, stuck in the cave of the dragon who had tricked her into it, and she was no closer to escape now than she had been on the day she'd been imprisoned.

The problem was that the dragon, in the footsteps of its father, was a good thief. The enormous cave was full of treasure, and much of it was magical. Too much. Every time Janell tried to find the thread that would unwind the ensorcelling on the amulet, she ended up at some other place. This last time, she'd found herself feeling a pouch of flower seeds blessed by some Druid to bloom without water. Very nice, but hardly useful.

By now, she reasoned, her home had probably crumbled to ruin or been taken over by some squatter, her thriving spellweaving business was dead, and her name was forgotten. Her only consolation was that in the ruby she never aged. Of course, she never ate and never slept, either. Her biggest danger was dying of boredom, unless one of her sarcastic remarks made the dragon angry enough to crush her, amulet and all. Or unless another wizard came along, one who was more powerful than the wizard she had defeated at this dragon's orders three years ago. Not that he had been a pushover--in fact, he had nearly killed her--but she had grown in power since. The one advantage of being stuck with this frustrating plethora of magic to explore was that she learned as she untangled the spells surrounding the pots, pouches, rings, shields, cloaks, weapons, shoes, cups, gems, and other ensorcelled objects in this mess the dragon called home.

She was a good sorceress. Although the amulet was of an old magic, she knew she could unravel its paths if she could only find them. But for that, she needed to be outside of this cave. Two times she thought she had found a way, but both times she was wrong. The first was when the dragon took her to the mouth of the cave to tease her with a view of the outside world. The dragon's rumbling laugh was distracting, but she set herself to concentrate anyway. Unfortunately her very effort to focus made the dragon think its teasing was ineffective, and it carried the amulet back inside, leaving Janell dizzy from both the sudden reunion with the magical channels and from the swinging of the amulet at the end of the dragon's claw.

The second time, which was more of a hope than a possibility, was when she finally discovered the problem with the knights. These armored fools came by about five or six times a year, trying to earn some glory, and Janell had at first been puzzled why they never tried to pick up anything from the glittering heaps of gold and gems. Not that it would have mattered, since the dragon dispatched them with ease, either with fire, tooth and claw, or with Janell's help. Admittedly, knights had their own focus, but they never even *looked* at the treasure. Then, while following one of the myriad dead ends, Janell found the reason--a thread soft as velvet, brown in texture, passive and not very powerful, but good enough. An illusion spell. To the uninitiated, the dragon's treasure looked and felt like so much damp rock.

At first, this had galvanized Janell. With the spell's warp and woof in her hand, she could break that part of it which covered the amulet, and when the next knight came along, she was ready. He saw what he thought was a ruby pendant, picked it up, and put it around his neck. Janell sent him a magical prompt, a desire to leave this place, but the knight was too brainless to understand it. He was also too brainless to hide the pendant, believing that this evidence of theft from the dragon would enrage it and cause it to fight less wisely. He was half right--the dragon got very angry. After it killed the knight, it was also angry at Janell, and Janell's hope that she would be put outside with the knight's body, unnoticed, was dashed when the dragon plucked the amulet from around the corpse's neck and snarled at it, "If you try that again, I shall crush you to dust."

Janell was subdued, but not beaten. She would simply have to wait until an intelligent knight came along. If one *existed*. After waiting for more than two years, she had yet to find one of the glory-seekers with more brains than a tick, and she was beginning to despair of that escape, too.

Her skill had developed by this time to where she could alter some spells, and she traced back along the verdal thread. She could make the enchanted seeds bloom and have a colorful, if short-lived, riot of flowers in the cave. However, just as she began analyzing the spell's construction, the ground trembled under the dragon's tread and she recalled the foolishness of what she was planning. The dragon had no idea of her magical work in the cave, and calling attention to it was suicidal. She withdrew as quickly and guiltily as if the harmless Druid spell had burned her fingers.

The dragon passed by, seen through the red glow of the ruby only in parts--head, long neck, legs, folded wings, tail. The faint daylight at the mouth of the cave was darkened, then became light again as the dragon launched into the air. Janell was still fighting the temptation to tamper with the flowers when another shadow crossed the daylight, one much too small for the dragon.

She was instantly alert, if not too hopeful. It was probably just another knight. Then again, maybe not; the man came in so close on the dragon's departure that he must have been hiding outside. He was a tall, well-knit man, with dark curls falling to his shoulders, wearing no armor and carrying only a plain dagger. Not a knight, then. But who else would knowingly visit a dragon's cave? Then he took a sack from inside his loose tunic, and the answer came to her in a rush of excitement. *A thief! A blessed thief!* If anyone would take an amulet and run with it, it would be a thief.

As he explored the cave, the thief kept glancing curiously at the shafts, which let in the sun. Apparently he didn't know how much dragons liked light. She hoped he wasn't equally ignorant about other aspects of dragons, like the fact that they never stayed away from home for long if they could help it.

He finally came in her direction, and she quickly banished the illusion spell from the amulet. He saw it at once, bent over and picked it up. She noted that his deep-brown eyes were wary and alert--far too alert, for instead of leaving with this booty, he was taking another, much more shrewd look around him. Then he put the amulet around his neck, reached into his sack, and pulled out a jar with a wax seal. *What is this?* she wondered, peering down. The man broke the seal and poured some powder into his palm, glittering white.

*Oh, no!* she almost screamed. She knew that magic well. It would dispel illusions cast on anything it touched. She cursed savagely. Once the thief could see what treasure was contained in this cave, he would be all day trying to choose what to take! And the dragon would be back any minute! *Idiot!* she swore, and prepared herself to perform some of the quickest spell weaving she'd ever done.

The blasted thief was thorough. He moved through the cave in a logical way, covering as much ground as possible with his limited amount of illusion powder. Each time he tossed a palmful onto gold or gems, Janell frantically restructured the illusion right back to plain rock again. The lesser stuff she let him see; even she couldn't work fast enough to keep him from seeing *something,* and leather goods and weapons he disregarded, eventually with disgust. He thought her dragon was a fool. She knew who was going to be the fool if he didn't leave soon.

At last he used up his powder and stopped in the middle of the cave, peering around suspiciously. Janell took the momentary lull to suggest to his mind that something might be creeping up behind him. He whirled toward the entrance, and she suggested he should get out of there in a hurry. He picked up his sack. It was almost empty, and he looked down at it with disgust. Then he lifted the amulet and gazed at it, the only apparently valuable item he'd found. Janell thought, *Why, he's rather handsome. Especially for a thief. Or should I call him a treasure hunter?*

Getting distracted was a bad idea. She let her suggestion lapse, and his own natural instincts took over. His dark eyes narrowed as he stared all around the cave once more, certain that he was missing something. Before she could begin another suggestion, however, they both heard the thrumming sound of powerful wings outside.

The thief moved extremely fast for such a tall man. One second they were in the center of the cave, the next just inside the entrance, pressed against the wall. The dragon came in and walked right past them, looking grumpy. Janell wanted to whimper, or scream, or anything to break the tension, but before she could do anything so stupid, the thief, with bag, amulet, and sorceress, was outside and creeping quickly down the hill.

Elated, Janell immediately started to search her environment for the red threads of the amulet spell. Away from the other magical distractions, it took mere minutes to find them, so strong and thick were they. She grasped them firmly and began to follow them, while the thief continued his flight.

The infuriated roar of the dragon made the air tremble. The thief cursed and began to run, leaping down the hillside. *Don't think about it, trust him,* Janell told herself. *Stay with the spell. This is the only chance you'll ever get.*

The dragon burst out of the cave in a hurricane of fire. The thief dived for cover, rolled into a rock with a grunt of pain, scrambled back to his feet, and kept running. Behind him, trees were uprooted and rocks rolled downhill from the dragon's raging search. Tongues of fire lashed like arrows from a random bow. The thief stayed low, moved fast, always downhill, panting and cursing in a quiet, steady way. And all the time Janell worked, worked, worked.

There was the obedience web, which had compelled her to do the dragon's will, heavy and dark. She lifted it, held it, and twisted it until it shivered, then sent her mind into the weakest part and dissolved it. Next came the thick, ropy, orange-red imprisoning strands, dozens of them; she separated them and pulled them apart one by one. The dragon's roar and thief's stumbling almost made her lose two of them, but she caught them up. *Don't listen, don't think about them. Stay with the threads.* She ached from the concentration required. Mages from the Old Ways had known how to weave spells that were intricate, one part bound to another, interlaced and sometimes even deceptive. But unweaving spells was what Janell did best, and she battled undaunted with this mage's design, following its logic one thread at a time.

Then she had it. The last warm, white knot. She held it between her palms and forced all the other threads far away from it.

The thief stumbled and fell. Janell was thrown down against the side of the ruby, and the knot slipped from her grasp. Her frustrated scream didn't quite drown out the sound of the dragon's steps and the brush of its wings against tree trunks. It had found their trail and was close behind. Holding two threads on her fingers to keep from having to start all over again, Janell forced herself to send him another suggestion. The thief acted on it at once, his mind sharpened by fear, and cast his sack as far away from him as he could. At the same time he ran in the opposite direction, just far enough to find a tumble of boulders that would hide him. He crept among them, and Janell once more turned to retrieving the pale knot.

The dragon found the sack, ripped it open, and pawed through the contents with screeches of fury. Janell carefully reached and caught one thread, the next, and then that final knot. With all her strength, she bent her will to it and shattered it.

The sudden change was dazzling. She was sitting on hard ground, pebbles digging into her rump; the air was hot. She could feel, she was breathing, she was *hungry*--her senses returned with a rush, and she grinned like a fool.

The thief was staring at her, mouth hanging open, looking a bit like the village idiot himself. She put a finger to her lips to warn him to silence, then began working a tent spell. It took her three tries--she was out of practice-- but at last she had a bubble of silence around the two of them. The dragon was no mage. Let it roar and flame out there all day, it would not find them.

A few sentences explained this to the thief, who was emerging slowly from his daze. She told him a story of how she had come to be imprisoned in the amulet, which was more sympathetic than true. Her own greed had put her there, but she would much rather he believed she had been naive. After all, the dragon was a persistent beast, and they might be here together for hours. "You saved me from a life of horrors," she concluded, looking up at him with melting gratitude.

She had already observed he was clever. He said at once, "Then I should be rewarded," and smiled.

Several hours later, having exhausted the immediate area, the dragon flew off to expand its search. Janell released the tent spell and the two of them stepped out into a scene of carnage. Together they raced up the hill to the cave, where the thief--her new friend--pulled forth another sack. Janell removed part of the illusion spell--but only part of it. She had not lost all her caution. They hurriedly threw gemstones and a few magical items into the sack, and the thief carried it out on one broad shoulder. One item, however, Janell herself picked up; a plain leather pouch. At the entrance of the cave she opened the pouch and poured its contents on the ground. Then she let her mind catch up the familiar green thread, and she reworked the Druid's spell.

As she and the thief walked away, the entrance to the dragon's cave bloomed with a carpet of flowers, wildflowers of blue, white, yellow and purple, growing without water or soil. Janell smiled at the sight.

It would be a delightfully satiric welcome home for the dragon, from Janell.

# Friends in Spite

I hadn't felt the cold for over a hundred years, but when I looked down at the corpse on that midwinter morning, I remembered how it had once felt.

A knot of people had gathered around the body sprawled in the snow of the village green, all of them shocked, questioning, frightened. In the shadow of Lord Arvallon's Keep, with his swords and soldiers to protect them, violent death was not supposed to come so close. I was able to slip away unnoticed, even as the village healer came running up, his gown flapping with the jerking of his knees as he plowed through the snow. One of the villagers called out, "No need to rush, Quinnel. He's dead."

"And has been, all night," said another, sounding as if she were speaking through a lump in her throat.

I kept moving, quietly, as unobtrusively as I could, but for once my sensitive ears were a burden to me. The arrival of the healer loosened their shocked tongues, and their voices rose with their fears.

"Who is it?"

"That peddler man."

"I want to know what killed him!"

"Wolf, maybe."

"Right here in the village?"

"Quinnel, can you tell? What did it?"

The healer's voice was cool reason. "I won't know until I can spellcast. Might have been a wolf, though."

I knew better. The killer had been one of my own kind. He (or she) had savaged the throat to disguise the marks, but I knew. When the healer did his spells, he too would know, for he would find little or no blood left in the corpse. The peddler was a vampire-kill.

Whoever it was, he was insane. That was the only explanation. Why else drink the life from such a man as the peddler, an unwashed drunkard? It would have been revolting to the taste, and the life-force not worth the effort. And to leave the body in the open, discarded like so much garbage! Only insanity could explain it.

I shuddered, then pulled my cloak closely around me, hoping that anyone who had seen would think me shivering from the snow-dusted wind. I had nothing to fear from any of my own kind, insane or not, but the madness that could come over a village when the people rose in a mob was terrifying. I wanted to leave, now. I wanted to be far away before the healer finished his work and announced to his neighbors that their predator was no wolf.

But would Trevia be willing to leave? She had pledged her sword to Lord Arvallon for the winter, and she never broke a pledge. She was my friend and my partner, but still I hesitated to ask her to choose between her sworn word and our friendship.

I'm a small woman, and I had levitated to the Keep a few times before by pretending the crust on the snow was thick enough to support me. But I didn't dare do that now, not with the suspicions that would soon be mounting. I didn't want to give anyone anything else to remark about me. So I stumbled through the drifts like any mortal until I slid onto the beaten path that led to the drawbridge and through the wall that surrounded the Keep. At the gate I pushed my hood back, and the guard recognized me and passed me through. Arvallon's own Guard may have been stranded for the winter on the battlefields of the king, unable to return home until the snow left the passes, and his defense mostly made up of Trevia's mercenaries, but these men and women were sharp and alert, despite having almost nothing to do. Between them, Trevia and Arvallon's Captain Virroc had taken the gaggle of disparate fighters, reminded them that they were professionals, and welded them into a force that would keep Arvallon and his lands safe until the spring thaw.

Safe from bandits and invaders, that is. Not safe from my kind.

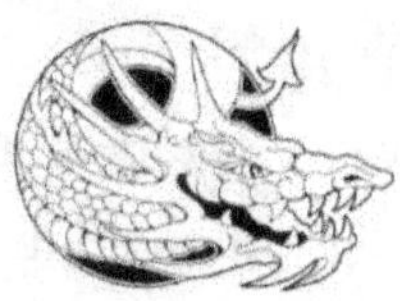

I was right. Trevia did not want to leave.

She has patience. She listened to everything I said, sitting in our room's single chair, knuckling her lower lip in the way she did when she was thinking hard. A whipcord woman, she was as tall and pale and slender as I was short and dark and plump. Her muscles were prominent and her hands calloused by the discipline of the sword. She was the kind of person in whom the blood is sweetest, running high with life and energy. But I had never tasted from her, nor would I ever do so. She saved my life once, and I had sworn the blood oath. Besides, I had few friends, and I never use them.

Trevia was the closest friend I had ever made since growing into a vampire, and I didn't want to leave without her. Since she was reasonable, she didn't reject the idea out of hand, but I could tell with her first words what her decision was going to be.

"You're sure he, or she, is insane?" She rarely used the word vampire. Even after all this time, she wasn't quite comfortable with my nature.

"He must be."

"Then can we be sure he'll stay here? Or will he move on?"

"What difference does that make?" I asked, but answered the question anyway. "There is no way to be sure. If a human goes insane, can you predict what he will do?"

"Point taken." She sighed, straightening, lounging back in the chair in a deceptively relaxed pose. "He may move on. In this weather, only drunks like the peddler go about after dark." She lifted her eyes and stared right into mine. "You know I can't break my bond to Arvallon. He needs us here. And I don't have anyone else competent to leave in charge."

"I know that," I said, trying not to sound as unhappy as I felt. "But I must leave. Sooner or later, someone is going to remember something about me. They'll recall the magicks I use are earth-magicks, that I never go with my head uncovered at midday, that I've glided across the snow--"

"Wait. None of that will be remembered! You've been so discreet, half the time even I think you're human."

"You don't know the power of people in mortal fear."

"All right, let me suggest something else." Trevia thinks on her feet quickly and makes swift decisions, generally good ones. "I'll go speak to Quinnel. I can do that without rousing suspicion. Any violent death is subject to Arvallon's justice. I'll act like someone who doesn't believe in your kind, who insists it was a wild animal. If he's unsure, it will stop there. If he's adamant, I'll pretend to be convinced. Then I'll tell him to keep silent about it to avoid a panic. We'll send the herald out to alert all the villages that there's a dangerous animal prowling by night. He might as well do something besides sit at the fireside and drink beer. If there's no prey for the killer, he won't stay around here, insane or not."

"And if he kills again?"

"Let's hope he doesn't. I'll handpick a squad of my most trusted men, tell them the truth about the peddler, and send them out to patrol. Can you mix up some of that awful stuff you use to repel them?"

She meant repel vampires. "I'll give you the recipe, but you have to mix it. It repels me, too, you know. It's made up of wolfsbane, garlic, parsley, and sour beer. Can we get all that?"

She grinned. Trevia's grin went up one side of her face in an appealingly childish way. "Sour beer, for sure. I'll ask the cook for garlic and parsley. As for the wolfsbane, I'm sure Quinnel has some."

"It won't keep your men safe from a straightforward physical attack, you know, only from being bitten. And not even that, if he's very hungry."

"He just fed," Trevia said grimly. "But don't look so worried. They'll have orders not to stand and fight. I just want to scare him off."

I had to admit it might work. The lack of prey, an alert and frightened populace, and a military presence making itself highly visible would have driven me away, if I were young and foolish enough to be prowling a small village in winter.

When Trevia returned from Quinnel's home, she told me that Quinnel himself brought up the need to keep the true nature of the predator a secret. Allowing the villagers to think it a wolf (as ridiculous as that was) would make them take all the proper precautions without causing wholesale panic. With both Trevia and Quinnel in agreement, I allayed my own concern.

But Quinnel was the next victim.

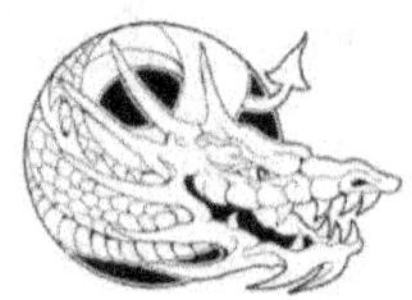

They found him the following morning, in his home. I was summoned, along with Captain Virroc and Trevia, because now that Quinnel was dead, I was the only person within a day's ride who could work any magic. The villagers' amusement at Arvallon's "pet sorceress" changed overnight into a demand that I do something about this outrage. Arvallon sent us, telling Virroc to "get this cleared up right away" and telling me to just soothe the ruffled feathers with a few pretty lights and magical-sounding words.

Quinnel had died in his kitchen, wrapped in the confining folds of his cloak, as if he'd stepped outside before being killed. Perhaps he had, had gone only a few steps into his yard to draw water from his well, and had let his death in behind him. It is a silly folktale that we must be invited into a house or be unable to enter. Bars and locks keep us out just as they do thieves and animals, but nothing is easier for us than to slip through an open door, almost invisible as a shadowself, if a person is careless.

Quinnel's throat was torn, like the peddler's, but this time there were questions. The village herbalist raised the first one as soon as we came through the door. She and Quinnel had been competitors, never friendly and frequently arguing, but she was sitting by his body with tears on her face. As the crowd parted for Virroc's bulk, she rose and pointed down at the body. "Where's the blood?" she demanded shrilly.

Once again I felt the memory of cold, all around my heart. It was over, all but the shouting. They knew, or would know soon.

Virroc was nonplussed, but his phlegmatic expression barely altered. Pushing past the old woman, he knelt by the body and pulled back the cloak to see it better. The herbalist demanded again, "Do you see any blood? There should be plenty, and there's not!"

"No. Maybe he was killed somewhere else, then brought here."

A man at the front of the crowd caught Virroc's eye and got recognition to speak. "Captain, I'm the one who found the body. There were no footprints but mine at the front of the house. When I found him, we looked everywhere for wolf tracks, but the only prints that were new were Quinnel's, at the well."

My guess had been right. Poor Quinnel. Better to have gone without washing for the night. I glanced at Trevia, concerned. If the vampire was cunning enough to have recognized Quinnel as a threat to his safety, he might reason that Quinnel's visitor the day before might also be a threat.

If Trevia had realized that, I couldn't see it on her face. She was staring down at Quinnel's corpse, her expression as blank as a new wall.

One of the men said, "What could have snuck in here and killed him and left no tracks?"

The old herbalist snapped her fingers at him. "What do you think? What would leave no tracks, and take all the blood? A vampire!"

There was an appalled silence. Then the crowd scattered and was gone in minutes, like a flock of birds startled by a loud noise. I could hear them calling to each other, dredging up all those old folktales, and one woman crying that she'd left her children playing by the woods.

The herbalist was the only one who remained. She was exchanging glares with Virroc, her instincts to warn her neighbors at silent war with his need to maintain order. Virroc was the one to give way; he growled something and turned to me. "Elianne, can you do the spell that could show us what happened here last night?"

I shook my head. "I'm not that learned."

Trevia had told him her own suspicions when she'd chosen her squad the night before, but Virroc was not a man with a loose tongue. "What can you tell us?"

Reluctantly I admitted, "I can read last night's impressions. That will tell you if it was animal or human."

"And if it was a vampire?"

"When I cast the spell, there will be a blue light for human, a green for animal. If it was undead, there will be no light."

"Try it."

The spell is not a simple one, but Quinnel's own herb closet gave me the ingredients I needed, and I piled them on the kitchen table. As I spoke the words, a ribbon of light curled up from the pile, straightened, and opened into a glimmering blue shaft. The herbalist said distrustingly, "Human?"

"Please," I said. I hate being interrupted when using an unfamiliar spell. "I have to remove Quinnel himself from the impressions." She subsided, satisfied, and I pronounced the second part of the spell. The band of blue light narrowed, then disappeared entirely. Nothing was left.

"I knew it!" the old woman said, more frightened than triumphant. She glanced down at Quinnel worriedly. "Does that mean he will--?" She swallowed. "Will he become a vampire?"

"No," I said without thinking. Her fear, and her genuine sorrow over the healer's death, overrode my own fear at the moment. I hurriedly tried to cover my mistake before the village would have one more oddity to add to my reputation. "From what I've heard," I said carefully, "it takes much longer than one night for that."

"That's merciful," she said. She turned her fierce glare back on Virroc. "So what are you going to do about this, you and that lord of yours?"

Virroc was unruffled as usual. "Everything we can," he promised her.

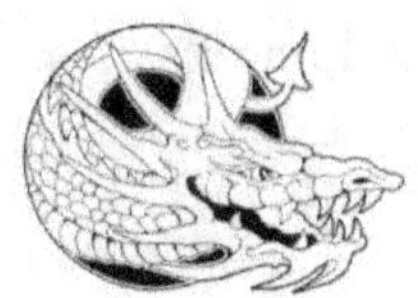

Trevia had said nothing at the healer's home. She didn't say a word on the way back to our room, and when we got there, she sat brooding for several minutes before I got impatient enough to interrupt her thoughts. "Now do you agree we have to leave?" I demanded. When she didn't respond, I said, "You saw those people. They're frightened, but sooner or later, they're going to be angry. Then they'll want blood for blood. They won't be particularly unhappy if they get the wrong vampire, and they will hang you from the same tree they use to carve my stake."

"We have to do something," she agreed without looking at me. Her gaze was fixed unseeingly out the window. "But not leave."

Her tone gave me a bad feeling. "What, then?"

"We have to kill him. Her, it, whatever."

"*Kill him?* Have you gone mad? Why?"

"Because we're the only ones who can."

"The mob can, when it forms."

"Only after more of them die. I'm supposed to be here protecting these people, Elianne. I know that's a difficult idea for you, but that's what I was hired to do."

She wasn't being sarcastic. My kind are notoriously insular, usually living alone, feeling no ties, not even to other vampires. "I do understand. At least, I understand that you took the bond, and now you won't break it. But I have to leave. If I go now, maybe you will look innocent."

"No, you can't go. You have to help me kill it. I can't do it without you."

My heart settled like a cold lump in my stomach. "What do you mean?" I whispered.

Trevia looked over and met my eyes. Her gaze was deadly in its determination. "You have to tell me how to kill a vampire. The real way to do it. I know all the folktales, and I've been around you long enough to know most of them are foolishness. I need you to tell me the truth."

The very thought was appalling, against every instinct nurtured in me since my birth. "I can't. I can't! I would be betraying my entire race. No one tells a mortal that secret. No one! I won't do it, not even for you."

"Then I'll face him without your help."

Trevia is the most stubborn person I know. She never starts a job that she doesn't finish, and she never quits. She meant exactly what she said, and that angered me. "You're forcing me to choose between you and my loyalty to my race," I accused. "That isn't fair."

Her face softened. "I'm sorry, I didn't mean to put it that way. If you don't tell me, I won't blame you, I swear it."

"But you'll still face him."

"Yes. Listen to me. Your choice isn't between me and your race, but between you and a whole village full of helpless people. This creature may be insane, but he's also cunning. He knew Quinnel would be his greatest foe. And he's not going away now, you know that. If he can't get victims by night, he'll start stalking by day. I'm responsible for what happened to Quinnel--"

"No, you're not!"

"I am. And I'll be responsible for every death after this, if I don't try to stop him."

My conscience was struggling like a fish in the net. "Let me think about it."

"Don't think too long," she said grimly. "It will be dark again soon."

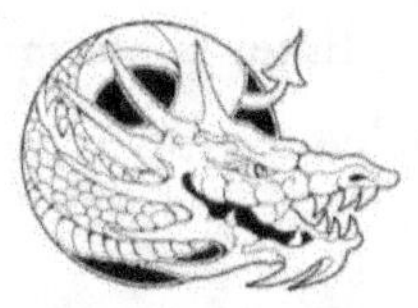

In the end, it only took me about an hour to make up my mind. I shapechanged into a bat and hung from a beam on the ceiling. I think most clearly in that shape. Trevia left me alone, going to Virroc to be sure they agreed on what to tell the villagers to do in their own defense. When she came back, I was already dressed again, sitting on the bed. Her brows climbed questioningly, and I said, "I'll help you."

She checked outside for any listeners, then shut the door and bolted it. Crossing the room to me, she drew her sword, held it toward me with the hilt upward, and said, "I swear to you on my sword, Elianne, that I will not repeat what you tell me to anyone, for any reason."

I smiled. "You didn't need an oath for that, friend. If I didn't trust you completely, we would never have become partners." As she grinned her idiotic, side-slipping grin, putting her sword back in its scabbard, I asked,

"Just how good are you with that thing, really? I've heard you boast, and I've seen you work, but I have no eye for those skills."

"You certainly don't. You thought that blundering fool Berl was good."

"So, how good are you?"

"Truthfully? Very good. I trust my arm as I do nothing else but you."

"You had better be right."

She blinked. "Your folk die by the sword?"

I nodded. "We die two kinds of death. If we are killed by burning, then we are true dead and don't revive. However, I don't think there is any practical way to catch this vampire and burn him. The other death is not permanent, but it lasts a long time, sometimes years. That is with a blow directly through the heart, delivered by something, which has never been alive. Like a sword."

"Not a wooden stake, then?"

I smiled grimly at her ironic tone. "That is the story we fostered after the first of us died by piercing of the heart. Wood, no matter how old, was once alive. We can heal ourselves of its wound using its life-force, often in mere seconds." I pointed to a chair. "Now sit down and listen carefully. You must hit the heart precisely, and unless this vampire is a gibbering idiot, you will get one chance and one chance only." I held out my hands to demonstrate my next point. "Our usual defense against a sword is to grab it and wrench it away, like this. It doesn't matter if our hands are sliced, after all. Don't think you can keep it from him, once he's grabbed it. You know how strong I am, and he may be even stronger."

She nodded, watching my face soberly, taking in every word. She had seen me lift and throw an overturned cart off the horses it had pinned. She would take that warning seriously.

"Your best chance is surprise, a single quick thrust. Barring that, then slice off his hands so he can't grab the blade. But mark where they fall! He will still have control over them, even severed from his body. Move quickly, as quickly as you can, and stay out of his reach, particularly if you take your chance and miss. He will be wanting your blood when he comes, but if he realizes your purpose, he will simply tear you to pieces in his anger." My hard-won objectivity cracked. "Oh, Trev, are you sure you want to do this?"

"Yes. Don't look so worried, partner. Have faith. Some of my original training was done with a man more than twice my size, and believe me, I learned to strike quick and neat and to stay out of reach."

"Good." I did feel better. She sounded completely confident. "After you have given him the little death, you can burn the body, and he will be truly dead."

"That's easy enough even for a dumb warrior like me to remember. Hack, thrust, and burn. And watch my backside. So, how do we find him?"

"We don't. How would you find a human fugitive in these woods?"

"Search parties," she said thoughtfully. "But he won't leave tracks, or even a scent for the dogs. Informants, but he won't leave anyone alive to tell where he is."

"And he can hide as bat, wolf, rat, shadowself, or mist."

"Then how do we reach him?"

"This is the really bad part." Enough of my emotion crept into my voice to make her stare sharply at me. "We have to lure him to us."

"How? Using someone as bait? How can we guarantee that he's hunting tonight, or if he is, that's where he'll strike?"

"You've answered your own question. No, we can't use someone as bait, even if we wanted to. We can't be sure of him that way. We have to lure him with the blood spell."

"I never heard of that one."

"It's another thing we don't share with mortals. I can cast it with just a brazier and a few simple ingredients. He won't be able to resist it. He will come to us from wherever he is. But the lure is the bloodlust, and he will come hungry and ready to kill."

"I'm expecting that anyway. What is the rest of the problem?" she asked perceptively.

"It will work on any vampire within its range. That means it will work on me. I can fight it, since I will be the spell caster, but I may not be able to resist it. If I am overcome, I won't know who you are. You will be nothing but prey to me. You could end up fighting us both. You may have to kill me." I spoke calmly, but I knew she could read my fear. I wasn't afraid for myself, but for her. If I was overcome, not even Trevia could hold us both off. She would die, maybe under my own fangs. I couldn't even think it, and I wrapped my shaking hands together to still them.

Trevia patted my shoulder. "I'll take that chance. I trust you, partner." As I opened my mouth to protest, she winked and said, "But I'm not stupid. I'll take some precautions. How do I break the spell, if you've gone over the edge?"

"Put out the fire. Kick the brazier over, even. Anything to disturb the elements."

"All right." She frowned. "I've got to do some thinking. You go gather what you need for the spell. Meanwhile, I'll tell Virroc what we plan-- leaving out a few details, of course--and find a good battlefield. And I think I'll pay a visit to the cook," she murmured absently.

*The cook?* I wanted to ask why, but she was already going out the door.

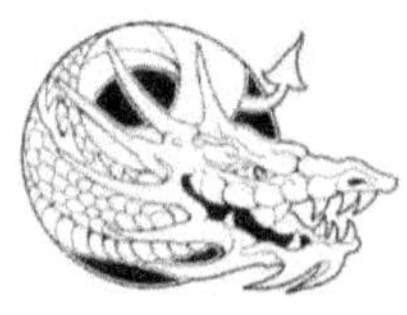

About a hundred feet from the Keep walls was a stone barn for sheep. Trevia had arranged for Arvallon to move the livestock elsewhere for the night, and that barn was her chosen battlefield. It was a good choice, protected from the weather and with a large level open space that was perfect for the style of fighting Trevia would be doing. Within the straw that piled against the sides, she hid several swords, commenting that if her weapon was knocked out of her hand, she wanted to be able to get another without having to go through her foe to do it.

She had come up with a good idea for me, as well. Once the spell was well started, I could maintain it with voice alone, and eventually it would maintain itself without my help. Therefore, Trevia brought a stout chair and chains to bind me to it.

One hour after the sun had fully set, I lit the brazier and began to work the spell. It is similar to a demon-calling, except some of the ingredients were different and no pentagram was necessary. While I worked, Trevia left for a moment, returning with a sack she tossed carelessly in a corner. I was concentrating too hard to pay any attention to it, or to Trevia as she began to pace back and forth like a caged panther, her sword drawn, her eyes watchful. But even she, a mortal, caught the odor of the spell when it began to work, and turned to see the first tendrils of red smoke forming above the brazier. The pattern set itself, and the rest of the smoke began to curl around it and then dissipate into the air.

"Now," I said, sitting in the chair. Trevia made short work of locking the chains around me, and I was pleased she'd taken me at my word. The links were strong and thick. Less worried, I kept up the chant of the spell, strengthening the pattern of red smoke, thickening and speeding the drifting tendrils.

It was seductive, the most seductive of sensations, the scent and feel not of blood as mortals know it, but of life itself, the vitality that pulsed beneath the surface of all mortals, the glorious energy of it. I had never cast this spell before, and I hadn't realized how potent it was. I was fortunate that it was quickly self-sustaining, for it took every fraction of my will not to be dragged into the sensation. *Use the mind, use the mind, ignore the body!* I ordered myself.

Behind me Trevia said softly, "I'll be damned. Here he comes."

"From there?" We had expected him from the forest. Trevia was facing the Keep.

"Right over the walls, headfirst, like a spider. I guess he thought we wouldn't be watching this way."

*I wouldn't have been,* I thought, and was grateful again for Trevia's wisdom. "Is he coming quickly?" My voice was barely recognizable. I prayed he was swift. The spell was working entirely too well. Trevia's voice seemed to come from miles away.

"No, he's dithering. He wants to come, but he doesn't. As we said, he's not stupid. Come on, you little bastard," she muttered.

By then, I was lost. Like a drowning person, I tried to keep some part of my spirit above the bloodlust, but my senses swamped me and pulled me under. I was aware of nothing but the song of life, the scent of life, the taste of its overwhelming, glorious, euphoric power. I could feel it on my tongue, in every part of my body, the sweet promises of that total surrender to survival at any cost. In seconds, I remembered nothing of myself, only that I was a being of power with a hunger. A great hunger.

My senses pulled into themselves. I could hear and see, but my mind ignored it all. The only thing that registered was the presence of another being, a mortal, one radiant with the life I craved. I began to salivate, turned toward the creature, reached --

-- and was pulled up short. *Chains!* I was caught up in chains, held to a chair like an animal. Trapped.

But not for long.

I smiled, gathered my strength, and let it surge into my limbs. The chains held, but the chair shattered like kindling. I rose, contemptuous, strong, letting the chains fall around my feet. Then I reached again.

The prey jumped away, but I followed, gliding, confident. It could never move fast enough to escape me. Behind me, I heard the crash of wood splintered by force; before me, I heard a curse. I paid no attention. Nothing was going to cheat me of this drink. I reached again. My hands caught flesh, sunk in, held. It weighed nothing compared to my strength. I pulled it to me, licked my lips, then eagerly sank my teeth into it.

And gagged. The blood was thin, thin as water, and cold. I gagged again, throwing it aside, as horrified now as I had been hungry. *Dead! It's dead!* My entire body convulsed in revulsion, and I fell to my knees.

Suddenly, like waking up, I came back to myself. I was crawling on the floor like a worm, a vile taste in my mouth. The brazier was tipped over, its contents scattered on the ground, the red smoke pattern broken and fading. Across the room, Trevia was fighting desperately for her life against the vampire we'd summoned.

He looked like a boy, shorter than Trev, slight, pale-skinned and dark-haired. But Trev's height and reach weren't helping her against this foe. She had missed her first strike and only succeeded in taking off one of his hands. In his fury at being tricked, he had grabbed her sword with the remaining hand, determined to punish her before killing her. This, a mark of the insanity that flared in his eyes, was the only thing that had saved her so far. She was holding the sword hilt with both hands, grimly determined, with no trace of fear in her expression. He was beating at her with the stump of his free arm, hissing like a den of snakes, and pulling and tossing her around the room by her own blade like a cat playing with a mouse.

I scrambled across the floor, grabbed the severed hand, and tossed it out the window before it could crawl over to trip Trevia. Then I snatched up a piece of the chair, one with a sharp point that would make a spear. It wouldn't hurt him, but it might distract him.

But even as I straightened, Trevia suddenly lost her footing. Numb perhaps from the beating, she tripped, stumbled, then fell heavily backwards, sprawling, awkward in a way I had never seen her. The vampire boy smiled; the hissing stopped, the silence fell heavily. He tossed the sword up so that he could take it by the hilt.

Trevia, a split-second away from being killed with her own sword, lay on her back, eyes open, unmoving except for one hand which had slid under a mound of straw. Even as I realized what was happening, the mound burst open, scattering straw, as she lifted one of her hidden blades. She coiled, feet bracing, shoulders leaving the floor, arm thrusting straight with the blade an extension of her arm, all in one movement too quick to follow. The vampire was just beginning his own thrust downward when the blade pierced his chest. The strike was perfect, directly through the heart. Without a sound, he crumbled, his weight almost pulling the sword from Trevia's hand. She held on, however, and rose to twist it, making sure of her kill.

Then she turned to me, her face showing nothing but relief and triumph. If anything, that made my conscience squirm even harder. Vampires can't cry, but sometimes I wish I could. I swallowed hard. I couldn't think of anything to say that wouldn't be asinine.

She grinned. "What's the matter? We won, didn't we?"

That loosened my tongue. "I almost killed you, you idiot!"

She came over to pat me on the shoulder, taking the makeshift spear out of my hand. "Hmm. I don't think Arvallon is going to loan me any more of his chairs."

I started to laugh, helplessly and maybe a little hysterically. "You are crazy."

"So I've been told. What do we do now? Burn him?"

"That was the plan." Still rank in my memory was the bitter, horrible taste of watery blood and dead flesh. "Trev, what did you do to me?"

She understood what I meant and pointed to the wall, where I had tossed my "prey"/ I turned and stared at a reddish, shapeless lump larger than my head. "What--?"

"That's what I got from the cook. Tomorrow night's dinner, a nice fresh haunch of beef." When I gaped at her, she grinned that sideways grin. "I don't know how many times you've told me how much your folk hate dead meat, unless it's been cooked to the consistency of a brick. I thought a little rare beef might distract you long enough for me to kick over the brazier. Of course, I almost didn't make it, what with Little Hellspawn there busting through the shutters at the same time. Still, it worked, didn't it?"

She was so pleased with herself that I started to laugh again. I laughed until I had to sit down, and she collapsed beside me. "You look awful," I informed her when I had the giggles under control.

She touched a split lip, a puffy cheek, and winced. "Thanks."

"How did you know I would break out of the chains?"

"I didn't. The beef was like the extra swords, insurance. You know me, I always like to have a little something up my sleeve."

"I'm glad you did," I said, subdued again.

She put an arm around my shoulders and hugged me. "Forget it, will you? I almost beheaded you once when you bumbled into one of my practice sessions. We just use different weapons, that's all." She glanced around, then sighed. "I think I'll let Virroc clean up the mess," she said, rising. "I'm exhausted."

"Do you want a ride back to the Keep?" I offered, still feeling guilty.

"No way. Anywhere we go, we leave footprints. Two sets." She picked up her own sword and thrust it through the haunch of beef, lifting it. "I'd better take this back to Cook."

"You're not going to let him serve it, are you?"

"Why not? Mercenaries will eat anything." She grinned at me again, giving the sword a hitch to settle the weight. "They won't mind that we tenderized it first."


End

# Just Until Sun-up

The two horses were the most beautiful Karra had ever seen, with bright coats the reddish-orange of steel pulled hot from the forge. The rough, two-wheeled cart was a good one, holding far more than seemed possible. She simply didn't understand how their owner could stand so calmly and watch them being taken away by thieves. She hadn't been traveling with Neieki long, scarcely a week, and she already appreciated the other woman's unflappable nature as a welcome contrast to her own. But this was going a bit too far. "You just let them steal it!" she wailed, as the cart and horses disappeared around the bend in the road.

"What did you want me to do about it?"

"Stop them!"

Neieki's green eyes widened, "How? Two of them had swords, and the other had a bow."

Karra stared significantly at the small symbol tattooed just below the hollow of Neieki's throat.

Neieki smiled. "I'm not that kind of a witch. I keep telling you that."

"You must have defensive spells!"

"I do. But to defend my person, not my possessions."

"Oh, I see. If the thieves had tried to take *you*, that would have been different." This just brought a chuckle. Karra demanded, "How can you laugh about this? Everything we own is on that cart! How am I supposed to earn a living without my lute and my juggling tools?"

Neieki bent to pick up her cloak, which she'd dropped in the first alarm at being accosted by armed thieves. "Perhaps we'll get it back," she said serenely.

This exacerbated Karra's temper even further. "Sure we will," she drawled. "I'm sure in an hour or two they'll be sorry they stole it and rush right back here to apologize and return everything."

The witch's smile deepened. "I'm sure they will be sorry. Or they will, if they are still driving those horses at dawn."

"What difference does *that* make?" Karra shouted.

Neieki's reply was not an answer. "The horses may come back. Perhaps as soon as tomorrow. Come, we'd better leave."

Fuming, Karra fell in step beside her. She could replace the tools of her juggling, but she might never earn enough to replace the lute. "Sure, the horses will come back. They're well trained horses, after all. But shouldn't we wait for them here, where they'll expect to find us?" she said, too angry to soften the bite of her sarcasm.

Neieki took no offense. "No, we need to be as far away as possible."

The peculiarity of her responses finally got through to Karra. "Why?"

"We don't want to be where people know us."

"Why not?"

"I don't want trouble. Do you?"

"No, we wouldn't want any *trouble*," Karra drawled. "We've just been robbed of everything, except what we have on our backs, we're unarmed on a road that's obviously infested with thieves, we're two days from the nearest town, neither of us knows how to hunt or make a fire without a flint box, and it's getting dark. I shudder to think what you might call trouble, so if you.... Where are you going?"

Neieki met this demand with a bland look over her shoulder. "Into the woods," she said, stating the obvious.

"Terrific. We'll add getting lost to our list of problems."

"How could I possibly get lost in the woods? The Goddess will guide me."

"I'd prefer the stars and a good road."

"You said yourself the road is infested with thieves."

"That's better than bears or wolves. After all, we don't have anything on us to interest a thief anymore." She hesitated at the edge of the road, unwilling to plunge into the green shadows, even behind a witch.

Neieki turned and beckoned. "We don't have time to waste, Karra. Come on. I want to be a long way from here by this time tomorrow."

Karra's chin jutted. "Why?"

Neieki sighed. "When I was given the horses and cart, long ago, I was told they were mine and would always return to me if a stranger drove them at sun-up. That's happened twice now, but both times, there was..." She searched for the right word. "Trouble. Just trouble. People don't understand. That's all I'm going to say. Are you coming with me, or not?"

Neieki could be stubborn, too. Being left alone on a darkening road was even less appealing than a hike through the woods. Karra followed her.

Neieki kept them moving through the forest until it grew too dark for them to see their way. Then, lacking anything better, they rolled themselves in their cloaks, in the lee of a great oak, and slept hungry. With the morning, they were able to gather food as they walked, but Neieki kept them moving even as they ate. Karra didn't understand Neieki's urgency, but it had infected her, and she forced herself to keep pace.

Late in the afternoon they came to a meadow, and Karra pointed. "I can see a road!"

Neieki smiled. "You sound as if you thought you'd never see one again. We'll stop here for tonight."

Karra had never really believed those horses would come back, and she was thinking with painful longing about cheese and bread and ale. "Neieki, there's at least another hour of daylight left. If we keep going, we'll probably come across a village."

"That's why we'll stop here. I told you, I don't want to attract attention."

"What attention? Who in the world hasn't seen a witch and a jongleur before?"

"Nevertheless, we camp here."

"Camp," Karra repeated dryly, "You mean roll up in our cloaks on the wet grass for another miserable night? Are you mad? Another mile might bring us to a bed, or at least a haystack!"

Neieki didn't answer. She was folding her cloak and laying it in the shade of a tree. "I'm going to find us something to eat."

"More herbs and berries," Karra grumbled.

The witch actually grinned. "Perhaps a root or two as well," she offered.

Karra groaned.

An hour later, with her stomach full if not exactly pleasured, Karra sat with her arms wrapped around her drawn-up knees, watching the shadows lengthen across the meadow. Neieki had gone again into the forest, seeking pine branches to bower them more softly than the previous night. Resting, without the need to watch where she was walking, Karra finally began to ponder the witch's odd behavior. She trusted Neieki, or she would never have agreed to travel with the woman, but she could think of no reason for this hard trek. After all, even if they did come back, how much trouble could a pair of horses cause?

The rim of the sun disappeared behind the treetops and the long shadows melded and became a gathering darkness. Even as Karra started to frame her questions: "Why did they need to flee? Why stay away from human habitation now?" she saw a flicker of light to the west. At first she thought it was her imagination. Then she thought it was the sun peeking between the trees. But the light continued to grow in size and intensity, as if it were coming closer, maybe coming fast down the road. Suddenly, it veered and burst into the meadow.

Karra leaped up. Incredibly, she was looking at the witch's horses coming toward her at a gallop, pulling what looked like a chariot made all of gold. She blinked hard. No, it was just the cart, their stolen cart. Yet it looked gilt, and in the next horrified second she realized why. It was on fire! The wooden sides were blazing fiercely, flames streaming behind with the speed of the horses. The horses were ablaze, too, their manes and tails banners of bright fire, their golden coats alight. Yet they raced steadily, without panic, tossing their radiant heads as if in play, while all around and behind them the flames made a blinding, dancing nimbus of light.

She crushed her palms against her eyes, hoping the vision came from something she shouldn't have eaten. Yet she could hear the pounding hooves, the rumbling of the iron-shod cartwheels, the jingling of the harness, the snorting of the horses' breath. The ground shook under her feet. She dropped her hands, prepared to either run or accept that she had gone mad.

Neither happened. The horses' molten coats were luminous still, but the glow was fading with the last of the sunset. There was no fire. There were just two horses slowing to a trot as they approached, a wooden cart bouncing behind them.

She stepped forward and caught the bridles as they came to a stop. They weren't even blowing, and they lowered their heads obediently to her trembling hands. Still... did she see a flicker of flame in their dark eyes? She looked more closely, but they were soft and liquid brown, the eyes of two good horses standing quietly. Shaking, she ran a hand along one warm, gleaming flank as she looked over the cart. There were no blackened areas, no ash, no sign of any burning. Certainly no gold. Just the slightly buckled, weathered wood, and, secured by unsinged ropes, Neieki's packs and her own, including the precious lute.

Neieki emerged from the trees, her arms laden with pine boughs. "Oh, good, they've returned. Is everything there?"

Speechless, Karra just stared at her. Neieki calmly spread the branches on the ground, then came to rub the horses' necks. "Now you know why I say they should never be driven at sun-up by anyone but me. Because otherwise they... run wild all day long."

"But..."

"Don't worry, they're perfectly safe now."

Karra swallowed a lot of questions and blurted out only one. "Where did you *get* these horses?"

"In the east." She glanced in the cart. "I'm so glad your lute is still here. Aren't you?"

For several long seconds, Karra stared at Neieki's round, pleasant face, with its guileless eyes and half-smile. Then she drew a ragged breath. "Very glad," she said, and left the rest of her questions unasked. Some things she simply didn't want to know.

Such as what had happened to the three thieves.

# The Sun God's Reading

It was a contest, you see, and Yula won. That's what started it all, or perhaps I should say ended it all. I don't know, it's too hard to tell. But I know that after Yula won, and got her wish, everything was different, and I can't even say if the difference was good or bad.

The contest was put on by our school, and the prize was the granting of any wish we had. We had to submit our wishes well in advance so they could weed out the frivolous ones, like world peace. I wanted a lyre made of gold. Don't ask me why, maybe because someone told me they played more true. Gunnie's wish was for a ship to sail the seas, naturally. She was never happy except near the water. Yula's wish was to meet and talk to Apollo.

I can hear you now, saying that wish was certainly one of the weeded-out frivolous ones. But it wasn't, not really. I mean, it was at least possible, at our school. If you aren't one of us, not a believer in the Old Gods, then you will never have heard of the school and will probably think this a fairy tale. That's all right, go ahead and think it. But the Believers know better. Their children, like me and Yula and Gunnie, are sent to this school to be taught the precepts of the Belief in addition to more mundane subjects. In many ways, our school is like any other, but of course there are special classes. And some of the Old Gods will teach those classes. I remember most clearly, even now after all these years, how I dreaded Causality, which was taught by Odin. I'm not sure if it was the one eye, or the way he seemed to seep grimness from his robes into the room, but he made my young blood shudder, and even now I blink away the memory.

But having an Old God as a teacher and talking to one alone are two very different things. That's what Gunnie and I tried to tell Yula. The three of us were best friends, inseparable since the second day of school. Gunnie and Yula had patience with me trying to draw music from any instrument that came to my hand; Yula and I stifled nausea aboard a succession of Gunnie's borrowed boats; and Gunnie and I listened with the ears of friendship to Yula's poems. The thing is, Yula was a good poet, a truly good one. But then I'm a pretty good musician, and I had no desire to play before that particular god. "The Muses, I can see," I told her. "They inspire. But in front of Apollo, I think my fingers would go numb."

Yula said, "I don't want to read my poems to him. I want *him* to read my poems. To me."

"Why?" asked Gunnie.

"I want to hear them done right. My voice is like a sack of cats. I want to hear them sounding beautiful."

I had to stop arguing there. Being a friend meant you didn't lie, but sometimes it meant you didn't blurt out the complete truth, either. And she was right--her poems always sounded better to me when I read them, quietly, to myself, than when she read them to us aloud. Well, for example, she almost failed Drama, which is hard to do.

Seeing she'd lost me as an ally, Gunnie shrugged. "You probably won't win anyway," she said, sounding both wistful and hopeful at the same time. I understood both. Wistful, because she and I both had the same chance of winning as Yula, about one in a thousand, since the contest was a simple lottery, and Gunnie really wanted that ship. Hopeful because we didn't think that talking one-to-one with a god was a great idea. They're unpredictable and powerful, and they don't live in the same world as we do. I mean figuratively, as well as literally. They don't always comprehend humans. Look at that Babylonian god who almost killed a freshman because he mistook a slang term for an insult and because he forgot that sudden death is no longer acceptable, at least not in a school. No one but very advanced graduate students are even allowed to be near him now. Of course, Apollo wasn't like that. He was aloof, maybe, but not known to be careless or dangerous.

"They say he's very human-friendly," Yula pointed out a few days later. The issue still floated between us, Yula being determined and knowing that Gunnie and I were still not convinced, none of us needing words to know what the other felt.

"He's still a god," Gunnie pointed out. "You never know where the reefs are with a god."

"I don't want to go sailing with him, I just want to hear him read my poetry!"

By tacit agreement, Gunnie and I gave up and rested our hope in the belief that none of us was going to win, so it didn't matter. We all three submitted our wishes, Gunnie with crossed fingers, me fatalistically, and Yula with a defiantly elevated chin.

The day of the festival was brightly sunny, with a few clouds to give the blue sky some interest and just enough breeze to float out the banners. Of course, that's all arranged, coordinated by Demeter. The gods love the festivals. They thrive on worship, as everyone knows, and at festivals they get praise and sacrifices from hundreds of Believers who, in their day-to-day life, never bother to enter a temple. The only thing comparable in their eyes is a war, but festivals are better because all the gods benefit, not just the warrior gods. Even the most obscure gods have booths where altars and souvenirs are proudly displayed.

We students were allowed to roam the festival grounds unsupervised, which might seem odd to non-Believers. But no harm was going to come to us in a place so closely watched by so many divine eyes, and because of the contest being at the end of the afternoon, they had no worries about being able to gather us together again to go back to school. No student would miss the announcement of the winner, not one of us, because the winner had to be there to collect the prize. Yula and Gunnie and I did the usual festival things; we ate too much sweet stuff, cheerfully lost money at temple games, and spent our allowances on things we didn't need. But when the bells rang five, we followed a stream of other students that became a river and then a lake as we pooled together at the East Field, over a thousand of us, all eager to know who had won this year's contest.

Naturally we had to sit through some other things first. Announcements were made, and smaller prizes were handed out, including a gold pin in the shape of an arrow to one of our friends as Most Improved Student. We cheered loudly at that, because all three of us had helped him study that year. But mostly, like everyone else, we listened with half an ear to the announcements (in case any of them affected us directly and immediately) but otherwise kept our attention on the Contest Committee, to see if their eyes glanced over the crowd and settled for more than a second on any one student. Because of course they knew who the winner was. The drawing was done a fortnight in advance, to allow for arranging the granting of the wish. It was all done in the greatest secrecy; in more than six centuries, the name of the winner had never leaked out. Still, that didn't discourage anyone from guessing, speculating, exchanging gossip, and then at the festival watching the Committee's least gestures like hawks watching for movement in the grass.

At last the big moment arrived. The Head of the Contest Committee was introduced and rose, and the constant low undertone of student chatter suddenly ceased, leaving the East Field in an unnatural silence.

No one could have been more shocked than Gunnie and I when Yula's name was announced. Except maybe Yula, who sat with her jaw unhinged, immobile, until Gunnie and I dragged her up and toward the stage. About halfway there she suddenly realized it--she'd won!--and made it the rest of the way without our help, at a dead run, not regaining her dignity until just before she put a foot on the first step onto the stage. Hugging each other gleefully, Gunnie and I watched as the Committee Head pontificated on the nature of luck and all that other rot, and then we cheered like Banshees when Yula was given her scroll and instructions. This last was done without microphones, quietly on the side while the brief end-speech was made.

When Yula rejoined us, clutching her scroll to her chest, her eyes were still wondering but her feet were dancing. Making sure no one was in earshot, she said, "He's waiting for us in the gazebo on the main grounds, inside the wall."

I picked out the relevant word. "Us?"

"Well, you guys are coming with me, aren't you?"

Gunnie and I exchanged glances. "That never occurred to us," I said.

"You've got to!" She grabbed our hands. "I don't want to go there all alone. You've got to come with me."

We did everything else together, so why not? "Will they let us?"

"I already cleared it with the Committee. Come on." She grabbed her bag, sitting limply on the ground between Gunnie and me, and groped in it through the festival stuff for the sheaf of poems she'd brought with her, just in case. Her nervous, clutching hands made a mess of them. I didn't laugh; on my back was my lute in its case, and I knew if I touched it I'd leave sweaty finger-marks on the leather.

We crossed the trampled green and followed the path through the little strip of woods that separated the fairgrounds from the walled estate. The path emerged just before a small wicket gate, and from there we saw Apollo's light, pouring from the deep windows of the gazebo, long before we saw him. We crossed that last stretch in silence, all three of us pretending to be brave for the sake of the others, and peeked nervously into the tiny, eight-walled building.

It was Apollo there, all right. We'd all seen him before, naturally, but at a distance. Yula and I, being in the arts, had seen him several times, as an occasional visitor to class and as the god who officially opened the College of Arts and Letters every year. But we'd never been this close. He seemed to fill up the gazebo, spacious as it was, not only because of his size and divine presence but also because of the golden light that radiated from his skin, like a visible perfume. It's always hard to look straight at a god, but the brilliant light made it even harder. We stood blinking stupidly, our faces golden in the glow, and stared from the corners of our eyes or from under our lashes.

He was lounging on a couch, and languidly waved us to seats around him, greeting us by name. We were startled by that. I mean, we knew the gods had ways of knowing that were beyond our comprehension, but Apollo knew our names!

When we were seated and had fidgeted ourselves as comfortable as we could, he half sat up and said to Yula, "You wanted to talk to me. That was your wish. What did you want to talk about?"

I have to hand it to Yula, once she was there, she wasn't afraid to jump right in. "I didn't exactly want to talk. I wanted you to read my poems. Aloud, I mean. Will you do that?"

"I'd be glad to."

She thrust forward the handful of poems she'd brought with her, but he waved them aside. "I know them," he said, and proved it by reciting one right then and there.

Gunnie just stared, and Yula, her arm falling again into her lap, slowly, with the poems still clutched and wrinkling in her fist, let her jaw drop again. As for me, I was probably the same way, but I don't know. I was too astonished to be aware of myself, not only that he knew the poem, but also at the way he recited it. The poem was a good one, but Apollo made it sound like the work of a master. He turned the ordinary words into beautiful ones and made the beautiful ones soar into the heart. When he finished, and the air ceased to vibrate with his voice, there was a long silence. None of us wanted to introduce the crow's caw of her own voice into the air after that. He smiled and said in a more ordinary tone, "Would you like another?"

"Yes, please!" Yula said.

He looked at me, and I jumped when he spoke my name again. "I see you have a lute. May I use it? I shall accompany the poem with its music."

None of us wondered why the patron god of music had no lute of his own with him, even one ready to be conjured out of thin air. Stammering, I dragged the lute from my back, took it from its case, and handed it to him.

He did another of Yula's poems, and another, and still more, until he'd done all the ones that she had brought with her and many that she hadn't. He accompanied them all with impromptu sweet tunes played on the lute. My lute! I had never heard the instrument play so true. Not all my practice and hard work had ever brought such beauty from its strings. I thrilled to hear it, so much that I lost track of the poetry in the wonder of that music that soared and flirted and danced in the air. My ear followed the tunes, and I tried to write them as they were invented under the god's fingers. My scribbles were sometimes right and more often wrong, but the wrong times were better than the right, for then, correcting them, I was led into paths of beauty that I couldn't have imagined. Yet when I was listening to them, it was as if I'd always known them, as if they'd come from my own heart.

When he was done and our time with him was over, he handed me back my lute with a gentle smile, then praised Yula's craft. He didn't dismiss us, he simply left us, in a brief flare of the golden light, which went blindingly white before fading away, leaving us alone in a now plain, quiet gazebo.

After a moment, Gunnie said, "That was really something, wasn't it?"

She was sincere, but it was so typically Gunnie that I wanted to laugh. I didn't, though, because Yula was slowly putting her poems away, her hair hiding her face, and I had a feeling that laughter would be a hideous intrusion. I didn't know why, when I felt like running out into the sun and laughing and dancing around for no apparent reason. But she remained silent, and her face remained hidden by her hair or by a deliberately blank expression. I did see tears glittering in her eyes, and I thought, well, they were her poems and she's more moved by the experience than I.

Later, days later, talking the whole thing over with Gunnie, I discovered something revealing about the nature of gods. To me, Apollo's voice had been like musical instruments, but to Gunnie, it had sounded like the strong surge of the sea against a cliff. The god had sounded different to each of us. But what he'd sounded like to Yula, we never found out, because she wouldn't ever talk about it again, except in the most casual way.

The other difference, the real change, I didn't notice until well after that. We shared a room, and I'd become accustomed to seeing Gunnie practicing sailor's knots and Yula scribbling on scattered pieces of paper all over her desk. Gunnie went on as normal, but I noticed that Yula only used the desk for studying now. I kept expecting to come in one afternoon and find her hunched over a poem, scribbling fast with her tongue caught in her teeth, or frozen in agonized writer's block, her hands pulling at her hair. But days passed, and then weeks, and still she didn't write.

Then one day I came in and found her tucking her special pens and pencils in the bottom drawer of the desk, on top of the special creamy paper she liked to use for her poems. When I looked at her curiously, she shrugged and said, "I won't be needing them, will I?"

"Why not?" I asked.

"Well, I'm not writing any more poems, am I?"

I resisted the urge to clean out my ears. "You aren't? Why not?"

She looked as if she wanted to say a lot, but finally she just turned away to close the drawer. "There's not much point now, is there? I'll never really be that good again."

That made no sense to me at all, and I said so, but she just shrugged the whole thing aside, and even laughed about it later.

But she never wrote another poem.

She did other things with her life. Married, had children, became a scribe for one of our organizations. She simply shut the door on her poetry, the day of the meeting in the gazebo. Closed the book on it, so to speak, and went on to other things.

Gunnie eventually got her ship, and it only took her about 10 years. She never understood what happened to Yula, either. "If Poseidon had come up out of the waves to show me how to sail, I'd be sailing every day," she said at the time, shaking her head like a baffled bear.

I still have the same lute, and I still play. These days there's not much call for lute-playing except at Believer gatherings, but I'm always asked to play when I go. I'm good with most instruments, but the lute has always been special for me since that day, as if I was inspired simply by the memory of Apollo's hands on it. And sometimes, when the light is just right, I can turn the lute and catch the sheen of gold under the grain of the polished wood. I believe I see it, anyway, and I remember that long ago wish for a lyre of gold, and Apollo's smile.

End

**You can find ALL our books up on our website at:**

http://www.writers-exchange.com

**all our fantasy novels:**

*http://www.writers-exchange.com/category/genres/fantasy/*

# About the Author

Fantasy writer Kathy Ann Trueman also writes romance under the name of Catherine Dove. She lives in rural Texas with a lifelong friend and a menagerie that includes horses, dogs, cats, and birds. She's addicted to chocolate, dragons, books, movies, and football. She's a 50+ single who graduated from a small college and still prefers the quiet of country life.

An avid reader, she was an Army brat who spent most of her young life moving, so books became her most reliable friends. Her favorites are fantasy, science fiction, romance, and mystery, but she'll read almost anything, even cereal boxes if nothing else is handy.

Kathy's short story, "The Sow's Ear", was published in Marion Zimmer Bradley's *Sword and Sorceress* anthology series.

You can keep track of all her books on her author page:

http://www.writers-exchange.com/Kathy-Ann-Trueman/

*If you want to read more about books by this author, they are listed on the following pages...*

# Greenspell: A Fantasy Anthology

In this collection of fantasy short stories all featuring female protagonists, you'll find diverse, imaginative tales, including:

- A sorceress unravels a spell and gets a result she could never have expected...
- A young girl wins a contest--her prize: to speak with a god...
- A vampire in hiding fears she'll be blamed for the reckless depredations of another of her kind...
- A minstrel travels with a witch who has a pair of very unusual cart horses...

As a bonus, this anthology includes "The Sow's Ear", originally published in Marion Zimmer Bradley's acclaimed Sword and Sorceress series.

Publisher: http://www.writers-exchange.com/Greenspell/

# Stories from the Vale

*Generations ago, ships full of refugees from a vast war accidentally blew into a narrow, sheltered harbor between the cliffs of two mountain ranges. The people called the vast and fertile valley beyond the harbor the Vale and settled there. The Vale was also home to wild animals, dragons, and magical creatures called elves...and magic.*

*As the years passed, humans with no actual magical talent came to be born with a Gift-- a single ability. Among the Gifted, only healers are widely accepted, but for others fear and distrust has led to prejudice, persecution, and even murder. Although elves, humans and dragons essentially live in peace together, the nearly immortal elves are intent on preserving the Vale's isolation from the rest of the world. At any cost.*

## Path of the Dragonfly

Shak is anything but a simple soldier with a clear-cut mission in life. He's consumed with the relentless need for revenge against a man who was once his best friend. But that obsession is far from his only. Shak can't forget he'd abandoned two helpless children during a battle. Though the deed that he can't forgive himself for happened in the past, far from changing, he can't get past it...until his grandmother, a witch, offers him the chance to redeem the dishonorable act.

Those same children he'd left to their fate are in dire straits. To rescue them, he must travel to the mysterious and treacherous Crystal Valley and then find a way to get them back where they belong. Further complicating his life, the Crystal Valley holds a secret that threatens two armies, and Shak alone can save them. With an unequivocal mission staring him in the face, he discovers his enemy is close by--actually following him--and vengeance could at last be his.

At a crossroads, he has no choice but to determine which task he'll undertake... and which to give up forevermore.

Publisher: http://www.writers-exchange.com/Path-of-the-Dragonfly/

## Gifts of the Elven

The Vale is home of The Gifted, those born with magical talent that manifests in unpredictable ways that many look upon with suspicion and fear. Even as the Vale's king works hard to teach citizens truth and tolerance concerning the gift of magic, the process is slow and politically risky. Many of the Gifted have no choice but to seek shelter in the stronghold city of Safehold. But is safety possible even there?

Sixteen-year-old Arlin is a nobleman's son, grandson of the king of Vale. Handsome and spoiled, he was born to warrior parents with older siblings who outshine him in every capacity. Misunderstood, his sullen attitude alienates his family. With the sudden appearance of wings on his back--a very rare and visible magical Gift--Arlin has no choice but to, literally, take flight to protect himself and his grandfather's reputation as an impartial judge of Gifted rights.

Fiella was adopted as an apprentice to the local bookmaster, where she discovered her passion for books and talent for sales. Her parents were killed when she was only seven--an event she witnessed that led to her desperate regret and longing to help others. While traveling on her first book-circuit as a journeyman, she impulsively offers to help Arlin get to Safehold, a sanctuary for Gifted, not realizing the danger she'll be placed in by doing so. Not the least of her worries is the secret she's been carefully hiding: She, too, is Gifted.

Shonwin is heir to the lordship of Kuturan. When he was a child, his father was murdered by his own wife. Living with a mercilessly cruel parent led to Shonwin's single-minded devotion to Kuturan. When the king heard of the ruthless horrors practiced there, he tore away their income and livelihood, denying them the rights other lords of the land were entitled to. To rebuild his heritage and birthright, Shonwin means to have his revenge. Arlin's Gift will enable him to not only discredit and disgrace the king but strike at the king's protection of the Gifted and his own beloved grandson, Arlin.

Publisher: http://www.writers-exchange.com/gifts-of-the-elven/

# The Rowland Sisters

{Regency Romance as Catherine Dove}

*For the daughter of a gentleman during the English Regency, life can be a whirlwind of parties, balls and outings--all to catch a suitable husband. For Georgiana and Cecilia Rowland and their friends, finding and securing the right husband is further complicated by misunderstandings, prejudices, rebellion against social restrictions, uncooperative suitors...and sometimes their own wayward hearts.*

## Book 1: Mr Harding Proposes

Eligible bachelor Mr. Richard Harding has his heart set on marrying his lifelong friend and neighbor, Miss Georgiana Rowland. However, the two have been good friends for so long that, when he finally screws up his courage and proposes to her, Georgie thinks he's merely teasing!

Georgiana has good reason to be so distracted. Her younger sister is about to be launched into society and most of the work and worry falls on Georgie. Also, despite her mother's furious command, she's befriended the scandalous Lady Shipton, which brings both blessing and chaos to the Rowland family and to their kind uncle, Sir Henry. Worse for Mr. Harding, Lady Shipton's charming stepson takes a strong liking to the beguiling Georgie.

Mr. Harding keeps proposing, again and again, while still trying to support Georgie in her trials. Is it possible for such a good friendship to turn into love?

Publisher: http://www.writers-exchange.com/Mr-Harding-Proposes/

## Book 2: The Lazy Bachelor

Mr. Peregrine Tyndall has often been called the laziest man in London. Even still, stirred to the enormous task of matchmaking when a hunting accident suffered by his cousin makes him realize he stands in real danger of inheriting an earldom--with all its tedious responsibilities. In his opinion, the perfect girl to marry his cousin and give the earldom another heir than himself would be their childhood friend, Portia Freestone.

Mr. Tyndall doesn't know what formidable obstacles lay before him in this endeavour. However, when he joins a house party at the earl's country home with this match on his mind, everything seems to go wrong. In the first place, his normally obliging friend Portia has a secret. She has no wish to marry the earl--she likes him very well but the man she secretly wishes to marry is Mr. Tyndall himself. An even bigger problem is Miss Frances Armitage. She and her little sister Eleanor had been left in his guardianship, a duty he has benignly and completely neglected up to now. A furious Miss Armitage is about to descend on Lakeford Hall to demand that Mr. Tyndall take up his duties to her and her sister in a responsible manner--even if she has to force him to do it!

Publisher: http://www.writers-exchange.com/The-Lazy-Bachelor/

# The Wynters Series

## {Regency Romance as Catherine Dove}

*Harriet and Sebastian Wynter are the children of a pair of archeologist explorers who traveled throughout the Mediterranean. Their childhood was filled with adventure, education, and even occasional danger, and they grew up to be brave and resourceful. With their parents' deaths, however, they are raised to adulthood by their beloved aunt in London. To please their aunt, they try to fit in with London society, but their love for adventure is always just beneath the surface, ready to launch them into trouble.*

**Coming Soon:**

**Book 1: Harriet Disguised**

Harriet Wynter is struggling to be a proper lady. She is successful, but she pays for it with frustration at her lack of freedom. When her brother goes off with some unknown stranger who claims to have a trunk that belonged to their late parents, she is irritated because he won't take her with him. But when he fails to return, she determines to rescue him, disguises herself as a boy, and sets off on the stage to follow his trail. Her resourcefulness will be tested as she faces kidnappers, smugglers, social ruin, and, most of all, love.

In a convivial evening with his best friends, Lord Ashurst drowns his sorrows with too much drink and passes out. His friends play a trick on him and set him, peacefully snoozing, on the next stage south. To his confusion, he ends up on a country road, without valet or horse or even a change of clothes, along with a young boy apparently running away from school. It doesn't take him long to discover the boy is actually a young lady, but he's captured by her courage and decides to help her find her brother. Harriet leads him on his first real adventure...

## Book 2: Sebastian Undercover

Sebastian Wynter returns from the Battle of Waterloo with a limp and a depression that even visiting his sister can't quite lift. He goes to the country home of his uncle, where he spent the summers of his youth, expecting to find peace. There he meets Eugenia, who is so shy he almost never notices her. His boredom is relieved by an old acquaintance, Payne, who'd once kidnapped him, years before. He joins Payne under cover to bring down a ruthless French pirate. He is aware of the extreme danger to himself, but never expects it to reach Eugenia. When it does, his feelings for her change his life.

Eugenia Slade has secretly loved Sebastian Wynter since she met him, when he went off to war. But she's an orphaned relative of his uncle's second wife, hardly more than a servant, with no beauty, no money, and a tarnished name - what chance does she have with him? She's too shy to even talk to him, and his only interest in her seems to be a mild pity. However, when she believes he's in danger, she finds her passion and courage run deep. Not only does she risk her life to help him, but when he learns to love her, she is willing to give him up for his own good.